T0132090

My Name Is Jacob and I Am Autistic

Mary B. Hammock, MSN, CPNP

--To MY Jacob and his beautiful smile
and my father, JEB, who reminded me,
“Jacob is still Jacob.”- -MBH

Copyright © 2012 by Mary B. Hammock. 107901-HAMM

ISBN: Softcover 978-1-4691-5381-0

All rights reserved. No part of this book may be reproduced
or transmitted in any form or by any means, electronic or
mechanical, including photocopying, recording, or by any
information storage and retrieval system, without permission
in writing from the copyright owner.

This is a work of fiction. Names, characters, places and incidents
either are the product of the author's imagination or are used
fictitiously, and any resemblance to any actual persons, living or
dead, events, or locales is entirely coincidental.

To order additional copies of this book, contact:
Xlibris Corporation
1-888-795-4274
www.Xlibris.com
Orders@Xlibris.com

My name is Jacob
And I am five years old.
I am autistic,
As my mom and dad were told.

I did not talk
When I was two.
My parents were frustrated
And didn't know what to do.

It was time for my check-up.
They took me to see Ms. Mary.
She is a Pediatric Nurse Practitioner.
Although she is nice, sometimes it is scary.

Ms. Mary asked a lot of questions
About things I could and couldn't do.
She called them developmental milestones.
It seemed I was behind in a few.

I could walk and run.
With my body, I loved to crash.
I would throw myself onto the floor
And onto the furniture, I would bash.

I didn't talk.
Instead, I screamed.
Hundreds of times a day,
Or so it seemed.

I would only stop to eat
In front of the tv.
I would feed myself.
But not with a spoon, you see.

I couldn't scribble with a crayon,
String a bead or stack blocks.
I couldn't take off my clothes,
Especially, my socks.

Ms. Mary told Mom and Dad
Of her concerns.
She said, "Don't worry,
These are things he will learn!"

"And please remember,
Jacob is still Jacob!" she said.
"Those hugs, that beautiful smile
And all the joy he spreads."
MS MAR
CPNP

Ms. Mary sent me to a Speech Pathologist.
She worked with me every week.
With her help, my first words came.
Then things didn't seem so bleak.

I also saw an Occupational Therapist.
She helped me develop fine motor skills.
This is being able to do things with your hands,
Such as eating without spills.

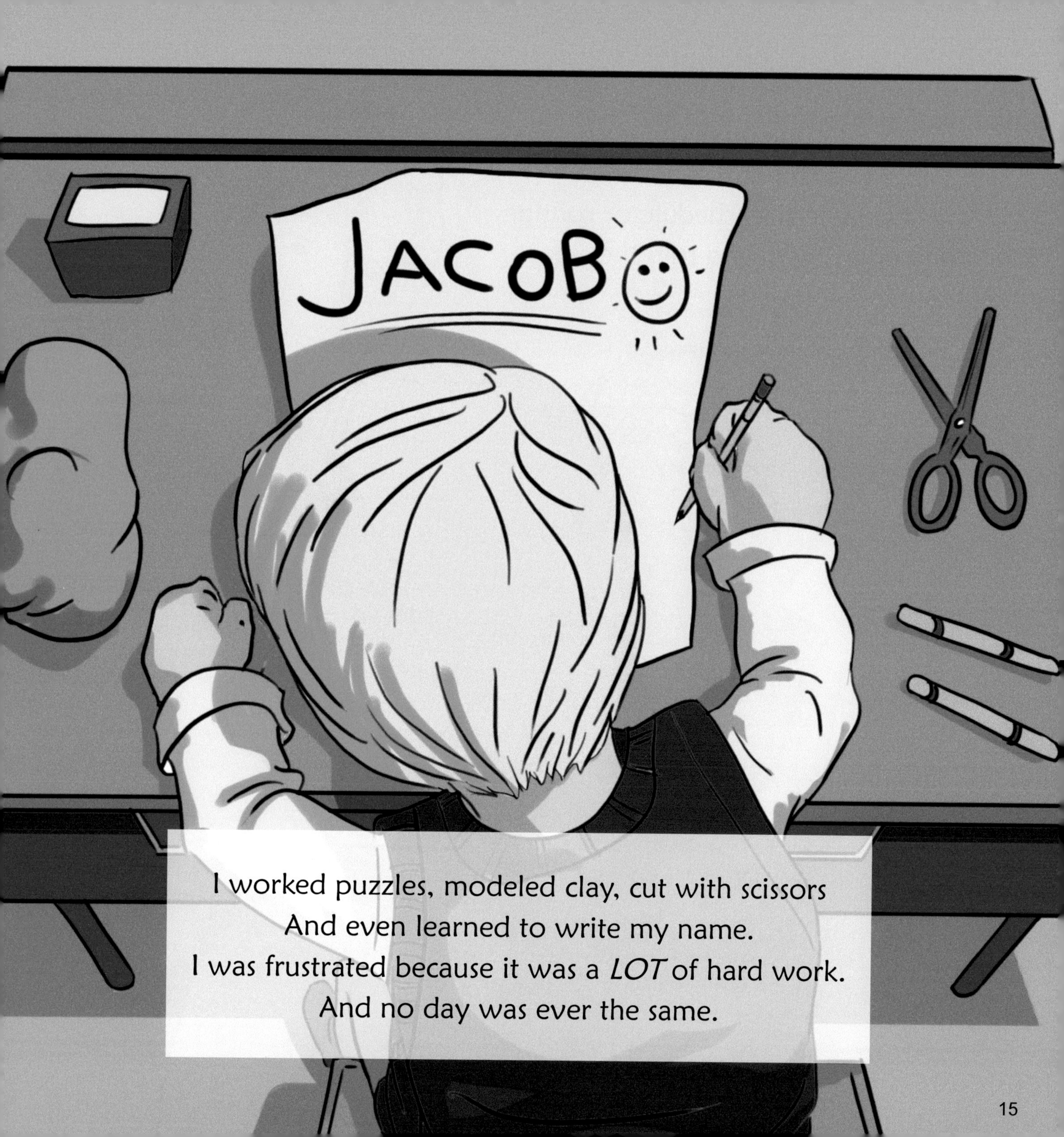

I worked puzzles, modeled clay, cut with scissors
And even learned to write my name.
I was frustrated because it was a *LOT* of hard work.
And no day was ever the same.

You see, someone with autism
Likes things just their way.
Any change in the schedule or routine
May upset them and ruin their day.

Mom and Dad know that one day
They will remember all the worry.
All the work they did at home with me;
No goal was met in a hurry.

Ms. Mary came to my Pre-K graduation.
I gave her a big high five.
She always believed in me
And made sure I would grow well and thrive.

Every year with continued therapy,
I meet more and more goals.
I understand and speak more words
And I am much better as a whole.

I will catch up with others
My age very soon.
I will do math, spell, read
And sing to the same tune.

Curiousity is natural
And a sign of being smart.
I ask that you be accepting
And open up your heart.

If you see me
Or someone special like me,
Don't be afraid,
Patience is the key.

Printed in the United States
by Baker & Taylor Publisher Services